GW01269813

The Twin Chariot

Jane Spiro

Series Editor: John McRae

Edward Arnold
A division of Hodder & Stoughton
LONDON   MELBOURNE   AUCKLAND

© 1990 Jane Spiro

First published in Great Britain 1990

British Library Cataloguing in Publication Data

Spiro, Jane
    The twin chariot. – (Edward Arnold readers library).
    1. English language – Readers
    I. Title
    428.6

    ISBN 0-340-52419-7

Typeset in 12/14 pt English Times by Colset Private Limited,
Singapore
Printed and bound in Hong Kong for Edward Arnold, the educa-
tional, academic and medical publishing division of Hodder and
Stoughton Limited, Mill Road, Dunton Green, Sevenoaks, Kent
by Cambus Litho, East Kilbride

Chapter 1

The Twin Chariot

The moon becomes bigger and then smaller. The sun is sometimes weak, sometimes strong. The sun travels across the sky, and usually when it finishes the journey, the moon takes its place.

Because of this continuous journey, many peoples see the sun as a traveller. The Greeks saw the sun as a chariot, a car pulled by horses. The son of Helios, the sun-god, drove the chariot one day. He was not a good driver, and the horses became crazy. The chariot rushed across the sky, setting fire to the world.

In a Polish story, the sun is also a chariot. It has two wheels of diamonds. It is pulled by twelve white horses across the sky. Some peoples see the sun as a boat, travelling from east to west. Others see the sun as a person. In the day he or she visits the earth. At night he or she returns to the sky. The Aztecs saw the sun as a great giant. He walked on earth at night, carrying his head under his arm.

The sun and moon are both travellers of the sky. To most peoples, they are relations: brother and sister, husband and wife. One story explains the journey of the sun in this way: that all day the sun travels to visit the moon. Their meeting is always very short. So always the sun must continue its journey.

This book tells us of the two travellers, sun and moon. The stories answer questions such as:

Which came first, night or day?
How did the sun arrive in the sky?
Can we really see a face in the moon?

The beginning of day
Some stories tells us that, first of all, there was night. The Maker was not happy with this. The Chuckchi Eskimo people of Siberia describe the beginning of day. The Maker asked birds to break the night. Two birds tried, but they were not strong enough. At last, a third bird tried and was successful. But the work made him so tired that he lost all his feathers. The story in this book is from Australia. Again it was a bird that made the first day. After that, people in the sky make the daylight. They light a big bonfire of dry sticks each morning.

Other peoples thought that the sun lived in another land. The Kiowa Indians of North America tell of Fox and Saynday. They travel to the land of sun and bring sun back. But the earth becomes so hot that they decide the sun must travel back and forwards. Then they can have night as well as day.

4

The beginning of night

Some peoples have quite the opposite story. Their stories tell us that first of all there was day. The day was so strong, so hot, that everyone was uncomfortable. The story in this book is the opposite of the Kiowa Indian. The Maker, this time, begins with daylight. To find the moon he must travel to the land of night. Here he learns to make night: he brings it back to the land of day.

Another story tells us that the moon grew inside the earth. A man found it when he was gardening. The moon rose out of the earth and into the sky.

Another question about night was this: why is the light of the moon weaker than the light of the sun? Why is the moon white and cold, when the sun is bright and hot? The Australian story explains it this way: the moon was still growing inside the earth. When the man found it, the moon was still not ready. The Zambezi people of Zambia have another story. The moon became jealous of the sun: it stole some of the sun's fire one day. The sun was so angry it threw some mud at the moon. The moon still has a muddy face. That is why its light is weaker.

The sun alone is too hot; the night alone is too dark. When the world was young, the best answer was found: half of the time there would be night, half of the time day. All the peoples of the world seem happy with that answer.

The sun moves into the sky
In many countries the sun seems very near. People see the sun as a friend, a real person: something very close to earth.

Some stories tell us that at one time the sun lived on earth. In Australia, South America, Africa and the Middle East, the sun lived for a time on earth. Sometimes he was a great king, like the Egyptian Ra.

When Ra became old, people were very bad to him. The goddess of the sky became a cow: she lifted him to the sky on her back, to escape bad things on earth. The Barotse people of Zambia tell a similar story. The Maker Nyambi lived on earth with his people. But one man tried to copy him. He was a proud and jealous man. Nyambi tried to escape him but he followed. At last Nyambi went into the sky. Only here was he safe from bad men. The Aztec people of Mexico see the sun as a god on earth. He died in a fire and his heart went to the sky.

The woman in the moon
The moon is like a mirror of life on earth. People see themselves in the moon. They see a human face. They see a person who changes like they do.

Stories tell us this in two ways.

Firstly, they tell us that the moon itself is a person. The moon is the wife or sister of the sun. For the Barotse, the moon is Nasilele, wife of the Maker

Nyambi. For the Greeks and Romans the moon was a young girl, Diana or Artemis.

Secondly, they tell us that a person lives on the moon. This person once lived on earth, but he or she left the earth. Sometimes this was to escape something; sometimes it was a punishment. The British tell of a man who carried sticks on Sunday. Sunday was a day of rest; no-one should work on a Sunday. As an example to others, he was sent to the moon. The people of Tahiti tell of a woman called Hina. She used to beat flour at night. This made the gods angry: it kept them awake at night. One of the gods beat her on the head. She flew to the moon. There she stays, still beating white flour. The aborigines of Australia tell us of two men. They had a terrible fight and both died. One went to the moon: the other went to the sea and became a fish. The story in this book is from China. It tells us about a woman who escapes her angry husband. She hides in the moon.

The sun and moon move across the sky: men or women, chariots or boats or sticks of dry wood.

Every story has its own reality.

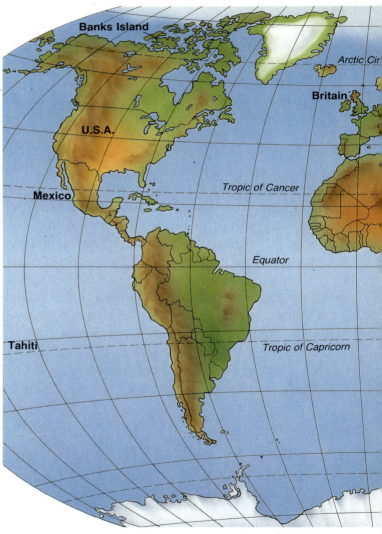

Banks Island

Britain

U.S.A.

Arctic Cir

Mexico

Tropic of Cancer

Equator

Tahiti

Tropic of Capricorn

8

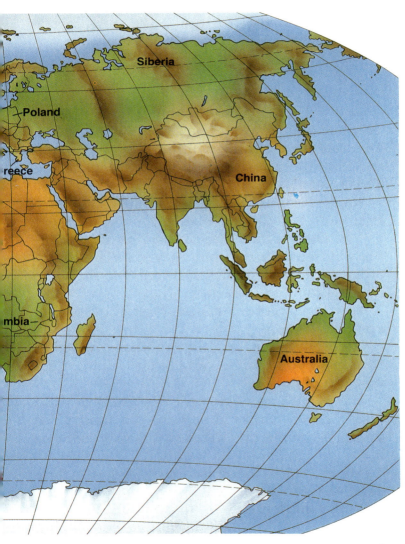

Siberia

Poland

reece

China

mbia

Australia

Chapter 2

The Beginning of Day

An aboriginal myth

Two birds sat on their eggs in the midday moon. They had long tails like brushes. They had combs standing high and bright on their heads. The day was dark as usual.

'Rather dark, as usual,' said the bird with the long legs.

'Yes. Dark for the time of year,' said the other. The wind moved in the trees. They could hear the cry of laughing birds, of animals running in the grass. But they could see only dark.

'How many eggs is it this time?' said the first bird, Emu.

'Three, this time,' said Brolga, the second bird. 'They were big this time. Not like my last two. They were easy eggs.'

'Oh, my two eggs were very easy last time,' said Emu. 'Lovely chicks they were. So hungry, so strong. In no time, they were away, finding their own food.'

'My two chicks found their own food after three days,' said Brolga, proudly.

'With mine, it was after two days,' said Emu. She

pulled herself up tall. Her throat stood high, like a tower. Her wings opened wide over the eggs.

Brolga pulled her eggs closer under her.

The time was in the beginning. The world was a child. Its eyes were still closed. The dark hung over all things. Emu and Brolga lived by sounds and smells. They found their food by listening to sounds in the grass, by following smells carried on the wind, by feeling steps in the earth. They knew the movement of every animal, how fast or how heavy were their steps, and how fast the wind and grass moved around them.

'My two chicks are so clever,' said Emu. 'They understand sounds in the trees better than I do.'

'Mine know the language of every bird that flies,' said Brolga.

'Well, at least your chicks are clever, because they aren't very beautiful,' said Emu.

'Well, your chicks are so strange, with their terrible long throats and long legs. It must be a worry for you, poor dear.'

Emu and Brolga spent many hours on their eggs. Their cries became louder and louder. Emu's throat became longer and longer. Brolga's wings became wider and wider. The eggs became hotter and hotter. Then suddenly Brolga lifted herself off her eggs. She flew across to Emu, wings wide. She lifted one round brown egg in her long foot and shouted:

'Take this, Emu! See if your chicks are better than mine!' and threw the egg into the sky.

It flew like a bullet against the dark, crashed against the wall of night and broke into a thousand pieces. The yolk flared out in sheets of gold. The light was so strong it burnt the corners of the sky. In seconds fire flared across the world and the night fell to pieces like falling rain.

At the time people lived in the sky. All this was a big surprise for them. Nothing like this usually happened. Usually it was quiet in the sky. Usually it was not possible to see the birds, animals, trees and plants below. But now the whole world opened out, like a marvellous painting. They saw silver rivers and golden beaches, colours as warm as the new fire opened below them. The sky-people stood at the corners of the sky looking down.

'This world is too good to hide,' they decided.

'This fire was a good idea,' said one. 'Maybe we could make fire more often.'

So they went to the forests, brought back sticks of dry wood and built a high bonfire. They set the bonfire in the middle of the sky. There it could light the whole world below, like a lamp.

'When do we light it?' said a sky-person.

This was a difficult question. Because Night was a good idea too. They asked Moon.

'When I finish my journey across the sky, I send

out a star,' she said.

'We will light the fire when we see your star!' the sky-people said. But it was not so easy. At night armies of cloud sometimes rode across the sky. Then the star would sit in the cloud, and no-one could see it.

So the sky-people made another plan.

The first Aborigine went down to the world. He walked through the grass and listened. He could hear Emu talking to her chicks. He could hear birds laughing in the trees. He could hear animals running in the grass. He walked through the trees. He walked by the water where animals stood to drink. Some sat in the water; some slept under the bushes. The sounds were quiet and sleepy. Then suddenly a new sound cut through the quiet. It was a cry of crazy laughter.

'Koo-koo-koo-kooriko!' it called.

The sound filled the whole forest, like an empty drum. Then it laughed again.

'Koo-koo-koo-koo-riko.'

The sound came back from the trees. It sent rings of sound out to the hills and back again.

'That is the sound I want,' said the first Aborigine.

He looked for the owner of the voice. He looked for something enormous: a body like a great sound box. He found many possible animals. Some had low, deep voices. Some were very quiet. Some could laugh, but could not shout. Some would not speak to him at all. Others made him afraid. He ran into the bushes and hid.

Then he found a little bird in a tree. It sat alone among the leaves. It had a red comb of hair, a long red throat, and yellow and red wings. It was the colour of the new fire. The first Aborigine looked at him, so bright, so fine a form, half hidden in the leaves. The bird pulled himself up proudly. He lifted his head. He made his throat long and firm. Then he called: 'Koo-koo-koo-koo-riko!'

The sound broke through the trees like a war-cry.

'Oh bird, it is for you I made this journey!' said the first Aborigine. 'What is your name?'

'Koo-koo-koo-koo-bu-rra,' sang the bird.

'Kookaburra. I have a question for you. When the moon finishes its journey, sing your song. Sing your song so loud, the clouds themselves can hear. Sing your song so loud, and then we will light the fire of morning. Can you do this?'

'Koo-koo-koo-ri-ko!' cried the bird.

'You will do this? When the moon's journey is over, call for morning. Will you call for morning Kookaburra?'

'Koo-koo-koo-ri-ko!' cried the bird.

Every night the moon makes its journey across the sky. Then the bird of morning sends out its cry. The

people in the sky set light to the bonfire. It sits like a lamp in the middle of the sky. At first the fire is slow and weak. But as the sky-people work the fire, it grows stronger. It burns hot and strong. It sends bright, warm light to the world below.

Emu and Brolga went into different parts of the land. In the daylight, their chicks looked even more beautiful. But they did not talk about their chicks again, at least not to birds from other families.

Chapter 3

The Beginning of Night

A Banks Island myth

Qat made the world very well, but gave it day without end. At first this seemed very nice. The days were washed with light. The colours of the trees and birds were bright as new paint. The animals spent all day in the water, where it was cold. For some time, everyone was happy. But then, it became tiring. Day without end was work without end. It was work without sleep. There were no cold places to hide, no dark places to rest the eyes. The night cats waited forever for the dark: the antelope ran from bush to bush, hiding from the light.

One day Qat's brothers complained:

'This sun is terrible. My eyes hurt with the light. When I close them, lines of light run through my head like knives.'

'It's true,' said another brother. 'My skin is on fire. Even when I sit in the water, it burns like a fire.'

'The land I live on is brown and broken,' said another person. 'It is so dry, I can grow nothing for my children and animals.'

Another person came to see him. He was so thin Qat could see his bones.

'The rivers are dying in the sun,' he said. 'The waters are drying into mud. The mud is breaking. This sun is too much. It is burning up our land.'

Qat went away to think. One of his pigs went with him. They sat under a tree beside the dry river bed. The pig moved around him, looking for food in the broken earth.

'I made a mistake,' Qat thought. 'The sun was a good idea: it makes us warm, gives us light and colour. But there is something wrong. It is too much.'

He looked at the dry river.

'There must be an answer. I must find night. Pig will come with me. We will look for night together.'

They started the journey in the midnight sun. Pig and Qat carried with them a basket of fruit and rice. Night lived in a land west of the day. The journey took them through endless forest, along the beds of endless dry rivers, along valleys of brown and broken grass, up and down high mountains of black rock, along long yellow beaches of warm sand. At last Qat could see the dark walls of night's country. They rose out of the water to the west, so high he could see no sky above or behind them.

It was difficult to find the door. The walls were too high and the sky was too dark to see. An old man came out to them.

'Your journey was long,' he said, 'you are tired.

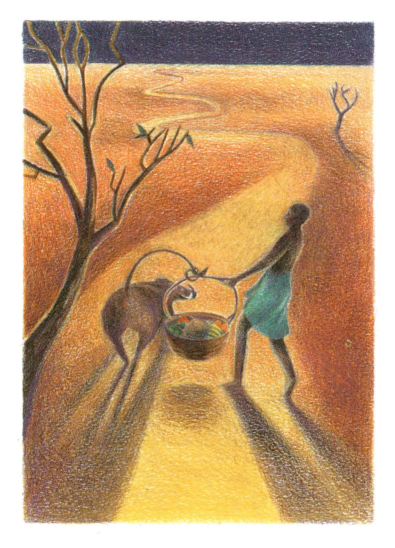

Come with me.'

Qat held the old man with one arm and Pig with the other. They walked slowly through the dark. Qat's eyes were closed, as in sleep. Pig hid his head in Qat's arm. He was afraid. Never before was the world so dark and strange.

Qat did not know where they walked. He could hear strange birds crying. He could feel wind rush by his ears. He could see crazy cat eyes looking at him in the dark.

They came to the old man's home. The old man made a fire. At last Qat could see his face in the dark. It was white, a face that did not know the sun. His eyes were strong and green like a cat's, but so small, as if closed in sleep.

'I will teach you about night,' the old man said. 'There are three lessons to learn. First, at night, everything is dark.'

The old man touched the earth by the fire. His finger was black from the fire. Then he painted dark over Qat's eyes, with his finger.

'Take the dark away with you,' he said. 'Take the dark away in your eyes.'

Qat closed his eyes. No more did light burn in his head. Inside his head was a quiet dark sea.

'Second lesson,' said the old man. 'At night, you must sleep. Inside your head is a quiet dark sea. Jump into the sea and swim.'

Qat stood by the side of the sea. It was difficult to jump. He was afraid.

'To jump, you must forget everything. Let the sea carry you.'

Qat made his mind empty. Then he jumped. The sea lifted him. It filled his eyes and washed his body. Then it carried him on. He did not know where it led him. Faces, animals, buildings swam to him, then away again. For a moment he saw his brothers, then Pig, then the faces of old friends. The sea carried him on. He lay back, and let it wash over him.

It was so pleasant. He could swim like this forever. Then a voice called:

'Leave the sea now. Your time is over.'

The sea carried him back to the beach. When he arrived, he was by the old man's fire again. He felt fresh and new – a new person.

'That was sleep,' said the old man. 'Night gives sleep to all things. But lesson three is this. We must end night. It cannot go on forever. We must call day back.'

Then he gave Qat seven birds. Each bird called the day with a different song. There were sweet songs like wind in the grass. There were loud hard calls like engines firing. Qat laughed to hear them.

'Call the day loudly, and it will come back to you,' the old man said. 'Now you must go back. Take the dark with you. Take the birds of morning with you. I will show you the road.'

Qat and Pig returned to the hot, dry land of eternal sun. The birds came with them, singing, jumping, shouting, dancing on the way. His brothers met them at the end of the path.

'So, did you find the answer?' they asked.

'Yes,' Qat said. 'Go and get ready for the night. Make beds from the leaves of coconut trees. Make them full and comfortable. Then I will bring you night.'

They made their beds. Then they sat in a line under the coconut trees. Only wind in the leaves broke the quiet. Then the sun moved towards the land of night in the west. It fell, as if sick. Its hot eye became weak. Its light changed to red and gold. Every minute the light changed. The sun fell lower.

'Oh Qat! The sun is going!' cried Qat's brothers, sitting on their beds of leaves. 'It is sick! Bring it back, before it dies.'

'Be calm, brothers,' said Qat. 'This is night. It will make you and the earth fresh. It will change the face of the day.' Then Qat pulled the dark out of the sea. The high dark walls of night rose out against the sky. It rose round them like a black sea.

'Let the sea carry you,' he said. 'Lie on your beds of leaves. Let the dark fill your eyes. Then sleep will carry you.'

The brothers were afraid. This dark was like

dying. But they lay down. Their eyes closed. They swam into sleep.

For hours Qat sat in the dark beside them. His brothers slept in a line under the coconut trees. Pig lay at the end, his head under a coconut leaf. The night cat was awake at last. It moved among the trees, its eyes like lamps in the dark. Animals slept everywhere in the forest, some in the water, some in the trees, some under bushes. Night birds cried and called. Snakes ran like rivers in the grass.

At last the time of night was enough. The seven birds began to call the morning. A loud new music called out from the coconut trees. Qat took a rock from the forest: it was flat and sharp like a knife. The night hung around him like a heavy coat. Then he turned and cut open the night, a long clean cut as fine as hair. The light pushed through; it pushed a thin line of light. Then the cut opened wider and the walls of night fell back. Light like fire burned across the sky. It washed away the dark in every corner of the land. The beaches opened out bright as gold. Roads of light cut through the forest.

And then, one by one each brother woke up. Their eyes were small with sleep.

'I went on a journey on the sea,' said one.

'I went on a journey with ten pigs, seven birds and an antelope,' said another. 'It was all so strange.'

'I met a beautiful woman,' said another, 'but

when I touched her, she disappeared.'

'It was terrible,' said another, 'I met my mother. She shouted at me for stealing apples. I never did steal them.'

Qat laughed.

'Now you know the three lessons of night. The dying of the day; the strange meetings of sleep; and the morning of forgetting and remembering.'

People walked through the day more calmly. There would be a rest from the light. There would be dark places to hide. There would be an end to work. And there would be more strange meetings in the sea of sleep.

Chapter 4

The Sun moves into the Sky

A Zambian myth

Nyambi made everything in the world. Everything came from his hands. He was pleased with most of it. He was pleased with the silver fish, the fast rivers, the dark lines of trees in the forest. The animals were like good children: they made their own lives but were always his family. They lived in the homes he had made for them, in the forests and rivers, in the mountains and the valleys. They lived freely, and let Nyambi live freely.

Only one thing was not quite right. One living thing he made was different. This living thing walked on two legs, instead of four. It walked tall, just like Nyambi. And everything Nyambi did, this living thing did. This living thing was man. His name was Kamonu. When Nyambi worked with wood, Kamonu worked with wood. When Nyambi worked with iron, Kamonu worked with iron.

'This Kamonu,' he said one day to Nasilele, his wife, 'there is something about him I don't like.'

'He watches our house all day. He sleeps by our fire all night. There is something I don't like either,' she said.

Kamonu, the first man, learned to make with his hands, just like Nyambi. He learned to build a house in wood. He learned to make nets of grass. He learned to make bowls of mud. He learned to make wheels of iron. Then one day, he began to experiment. He experimented in wood. He made wood in the form of man. He made wood as fine as a hair, as sharp as a knife. He made fires from wood. He made pipes that sang. He made carpets and baskets in grass. Then he turned to iron. The strength of the iron was exciting. It was so strong he could not bend it, could not break it. When he dropped it, it made valleys in the earth.

'This iron will make me strong,' he thought.

Then he made a long, strong bar of iron, and he made the end as sharp as a knife. When he threw the iron into trees, it stopped there.

'I can be king over the animals,' he thought. 'King even over Nyambi the Maker.'

In the dark, through the trees, an animal waited. For one moment, it did not know where to run: forwards or backwards. In that moment, Kamonu pulled back his arm. He threw the spear through the trees. It flew straight through the dark, into the side of the animal.

Nyambi was angry beyond words. Nasilele was sick with sadness. Nyambi shouted at Kamonu:

'These animals live in your home. They are your

family. To kill them is to kill yourself. As you kill, they will kill. Get out of my kingdom. Get out of this place which once was good: where all things lived side by side. There is no room here for you.'

Kamonu went away, but not for long. He knew the Maker could not turn him away forever. He went back to Nyambi's home.

'I am not happy to see you,' Nyambi said, 'but I have thought about you. I have made a garden for you. You are clever; you are quick; you are strong. Use these things to make, not to break. Build your garden better. Make the garden your own kingdom. And leave my kingdom alone.'

Kamonu lived in the garden with his wife, children and dog. For some time they were happy. They worked together on the land and the plants, flowers and fruits grew strong and healthy. Kamonu felt it was his own kingdom, and he was the king.

Then one night, his kingdom was attacked. He was sleeping when it happened. The sound of breaking wood woke him. He could hear heavy footsteps outside, the sound of running, of low, loud breathing. He jumped from his bed. By the wall was his spear. He slept with the spear beside him. He carried it everywhere, though never again had he used it. Then he ran into the garden.

Three large heavy buffalo ran among the plants and trees. The plants lay broken under their feet. Kamonu stood like a king above his army. He lifted the spear and threw it into the side of the buffalo. He hit first one, then two, then three. His throw was straight and strong. The buffalo crashed like great black stones, onto the grass.

Then everything went wrong in Kamonu's kingdom. His dog died. He found it one day under a tree, its neck broken. Then the pot of milk broke and the milk for the summer months spread over the floor and disappeared into the mud.

And then, one day, after working in the fields, his child lay down. He sat and lay his head on the grass and never got up again.

Kamonu went to Nyambi's house. The door was open and he went inside. There was a strange quiet in the room. He felt that Nyambi was watching him. He looked around the room. On the table was a pot, a round mud pot, just like his own. He went closer. He touched it. It had grass built in lines into the mud, just like his own. He lifted it to the light. It was his own! His broken pot, made whole by Nyambi.

'Yes, Nyambi. I understand. You are the Maker. I can only copy, but I cannot make as you do.'

Then he saw his dog. His dog stood in the doorway. Its eyes were bright, its ears high.

'My dog! Whole and healthy! Yes Nyambi, you are king and I am only a poor soldier in your army.'

And then his child ran to him, through the open door.

But this only made Kamonu more proud, more strong, more jealous of Nyambi's power. And it made Nyambi angry and afraid.

'Kamonu is teaching all men the art of the spear. He is teaching his children to be proud and jealous. He finds his way to our home. He finds us here, learns our ways, and uses them among men to hurt and kill.'

In the night they moved away from their house in the forest. Carrying everything with them, they moved across the river, to an island in the middle of fast waters.

But Kamonu learned to build a boat of wood and grass. He learned to ride the waters, to move with the fish, between the rocks. When Nasilele woke in the morning, he was there sleeping by their fire.

'There will not be war between us,' Nyambi said. 'But I will not live in his world. He has given death to the family of men and women. He has become the maker of bad.'

This time Nyambi built a mountain for his family. He put rock upon rock until they touched the clouds. Then in the night he and his family climbed to the top. Their home sat in the clouds. The family of men and women were way below, as small as spiders running in the grass.

'Here at last we are safe,' said Nyambi.

Nyambi and Nasilele slept happily. Clouds moved

across the rocks, and hung on their rooftop. Birds flew below them.

When they woke up, Kamonu was there, sleeping by their fire.

'This man will finish me!' cried Nyambi. 'Where can we escape you?! Where can we go where you will not follow? Is it not enough that you bring death to men and women? Must you bring your wrongs to us too?'

Nyambi and Nasilele were at the end of hope. The world had nowhere else to give them. Mountain, forest and water were not enough. The worst of men would find them in every place.

Then one day, Nyambi knew the answer.

'Go to Spider. Let Spider make you a ladder as fine as hair, to take you to sky. Let Spider save you.'

Spider was a small thing. Nyambi had made Spider in half an hour. Spider was a quick thought, after finishing birds, plants and buffalo. Now he turned to Spider, to save him.

Spider sat on the rock, beside Nyambi's house. He worked, with all his arms and legs. He worked through the night, sending up a line like smoke lifting. It was so fine, it could not be seen. It appeared only when light hit its side, and made it shine. The light spread down it like a drop of falling water.

After three days and nights the ladder was finished. Nyambi, Nasilele, their children and all

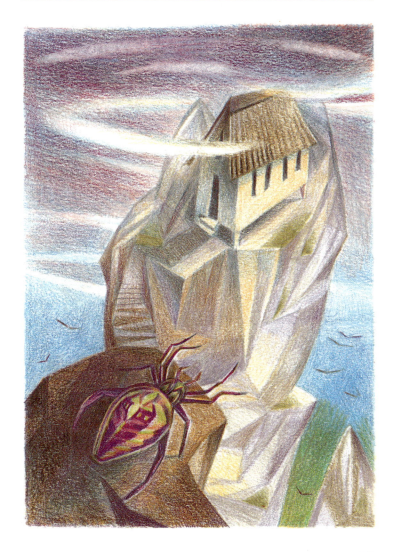

their household, travelled up the ladder. Even their house on the highest rock disappeared below them.

Kamonu built a ladder too. A hundred men worked with him, cutting down the forest. They put tree on tree on tree. Kamonu worked until his hands and feet were cut and red. But this time, Nyambi's power was greater. Kamonu could not copy the ladder of Spider. His ladder was heavy, unsafe, rough and clumsy. After three days and nights, the ladder was bending: the top hung down like a dying flower. The bottom bent and pushed out. In two seconds the whole tower crashed to the earth.

'Alright, Nyambi, I cannot follow you. You win,' said Kamonu. He went back to his garden. His kingdom now seemed very small, very poor.

Nyambi and Nasilele moved into the sky. Nyambi was bright, a round eye of fire. Every day he moved high above the highest rock and looked down to his people. They ran like spiders below him in the grass. His bright burning eye washed them with light. At night, Nasilele left her home to look down. Hers was a white, quiet light. Every night her light changed. Sometimes she was so sad, that her face was dark.

The sun and the moon once lived on earth. It was their first home. Then they found a better place, where the works of men could not find them.

Chapter 5

Chang-o, the Woman in the Moon

A Chinese myth

Chang-o and Yi lived above the rice fields. The fields fell in steps of water down to the valley. From Chang-o's window, she could see the hat of the farmer. The farmer walked slowly among the walls of mud. He stood with his feet in the water, and bent over the fields. Chang-o watched him. She watched the wide sky change from red to blue, blue to red again, and she watched the farmer walk down the steps of water. Down the steps. Then slowly up again.

At midnight Yi came home. His hair was wet from the rains. His feet were red from walking.

'I am tired, Chang-o. Ask me no questions tonight. Give me some tea.'

He took off his shoes, and sat on the floor. One small ring of light played in the room. He sat in the light and drank tea. Chang-o sat in the dark and watched. His eyes never looked at her.

'You are hiding something,' she said. He laughed coldly.

'Why do you think that?'

'Because you won't look at me.'

He lifted his eyes from the tea. They were dark and distant. Then he took from under his coat a small bottle. He put it in the ring of light.

'I brought this back from my journey. I travelled mountains, forests and fields of rice to find this. The bottle is nothing: a piece of mud. But what is inside the bottle is without price.'

'What is that, in the bottle?'

'The juice of fruit, found on the highest mountain, juice pressed from the sweetest flowers, the waters drawn from the fastest rivers and deepest wells, the blood of the strongest animals, kings of the forest.'

'And what good is all that?'

'Ask me no more questions. Give me more tea.'

All night Yi sat by the bottle. The bottle sat in the ring of light, Yi beside it.

'Sleep Yi, you are tired,' Chang-o said.

But his eyes were dark and distant. He did not move, did not sleep, did not speak. The light played through the bottle.

'What is that bottle, Yi, that you must watch it like a dying child?' cried Chang-o.

'What is inside the bottle is without price,' he answered. 'I must watch it, so it does not go away.'

'That is crazy. How can a bottle go away? Sleep now, Yi.'

But Yi never listened. He sat until the room

became red with the beginning of day. He sat until the bottle was washed with sunlight. Then he stood up.

'I will put the bottle where no-one can find it. When I return, I will watch it again.'

'Are you crazy!' cried Chang-o. 'To do this for a cup of muddy river water. The sun has touched you.'

He pushed her away. When angry he would not talk to her. He would not look at her. His eyes would be cold and distant. She could not live with him when he was angry. It was too lonely.

When Yi was out, she looked for the bottle. She looked under the carpets; she looked behind the doors, inside the large bowls and cups in the kitchen, inside the heads of flowers, under the water of the rice fields. The wide sky changed from blue to red. The moon moved into the sky like a large laughing eye.

Then Yi came home.

'Give me some tea,' he said.

When Chang-o came to him with tea, he was sitting on the floor. The bottle was beside him.

'What is it in that bottle? Why is it so important to you?' she asked.

'The waters of a thousand rivers are in that bottle,' he said.

'You do not give me the real answer,' she said. 'I

will wait until you give me the real answer.'

The moon sent a ring of light into the room. The hours passed by and the moon moved in the clouds. Yi sat by the bottle, Chang-o beside him. Hours passed. The ring of light became bigger. The light became redder. Then Chang-o said:

'We have passed a whole night with the moon. Will you tell me the answer now?'

Yi looked up. His eyes were dark and distant.

'The answer is this. Inside the bottle is the juice of eternal life. The person who drinks this juice will live forever.'

'And you hide this juice from me?'

'I hide it from all people in this world. It is without price.'

In the morning, Chang-o sat at the window. The farmer bent over the rice fields. He walked from step to step of water. The sun sent lines of light along the water.

She waited until Yi was away, until she could no longer see the top of his hat through the trees. Then she stood up. It was not under the carpets. It was not in the flower-heads. It was not under the bowls or behind the pots. It was not under the water. It was in the wall of mud. Yi had opened the mud, and put the bottle inside. There it was cold; it was washed by new water. It was watched all day by the farmer. The farmer who knew nothing.

When the sun was at its highest, the farmer stopped work. He sat in his hut in the middle of the field. For one hour, he slept and drank tea. This was the time for Chang-o. She took off her shoes. Her feet stood deep in the warm water. Then she walked along the wall of mud.

It was built round and high. It shone with new rain. Then near the end of the wall Chang-o found a stone. A round white stone. It sat on the mud, as if dropped from the moon. It was flat, as if washed for many years by fast waters.

'This stone does not come from the rice fields. This is a stone that lived on river beds. A stone Yi brought back with him from his journey. This stone is Yi's sign: here lies the cup of life.'

She bent quickly and opened the mud with her fingers. The bottle was there, washed clean and cold.

'Here's to life!' she cried.

And then, with one movement, she sent all its sweet strong juice running down her throat. It spread like tongues of fire through her body.

'I will be young forever! I will be as old as the sun, as new as the moon. Like the sun I will never change, never lose my colour. Like the moon, I will change and become new, every day of my life!'

But there was one more thing to do. She took the bottle and bent over the field. It filled to the top with the dark muddy water.

'There! You will never know the difference! You, who think yourself so important, so clever, so different. This is the cup of life for you!'

Then she put the bottle back into the mud. Closed the mud carefully over the bottle. Put the moonstone back in its place. And walked slowly back to her home.

Yi came home when the moon was high.

'Give me some tea,' he said.

He drank his tea in the ring of light. Chang-o sat quietly beside him.

'You know nothing of my real life,' she thought. 'You sit beside me and do not see how I have changed. You look at me, but see only yourself. What I have done is my answer to you.'

The bottle sat beside Yi. The light played through it. She could see the line of water inside.

'You will watch the bottle tonight,' said Yi at last.

'I will not. Tonight I will sleep.'

'Tonight you will watch the bottle. Because it interests me no longer.'

He turned to her. His eyes sent ice into her heart.

'You will watch it because it is yours. It is mud and water, of no worth. You have laughed at me, stolen from me, made my gifts cheap. There was no richer gift, no greater price than the one I paid. And you laughed at it. You threw it away and left not a drop for me. There can be nothing left for us.'

Chang-o tried to say, 'I made a terrible mistake', but no words came. She tried to touch his arm, but she could not move. His anger turned her to ice.

She sat by the bottle filled with muddy water. The moon threw a line of light into the room.

'Maybe I will live forever,' she thought. 'But do I want to? To live forever like this?' The moon passed through the clouds. Its face was white and full. It stayed like a great round plate above the rice fields.

'It looks so quiet, so calm up there,' she thought.

The hours moved into deep night. Yi slept on the carpet. His anger would always be there. There would never be calm again, here in this room.

The moon sent rings of light into the room. They moved around Chang-o. They made a carpet under her. They touched her hair and face, built a net of light around her. The face of Chang-o moved with the moon in the morning. The moon sent its last light into the room where Yi still lay sleeping on the carpet.

Glossary

basket   a bag made of bent sticks or dry grass
breathing   taking air into the body
bush   small low tree in open country
to climb   to go upwards
coconut   a round hard fruit
comb   the bright colours on a bird's head
drum   a musical instrument made of wood and skin
earth   (1) the world where we live (2) the land, where trees and flowers grow
eternal   to last forever
to experiment   to try something new
giant   an enormous person
to grow   to become bigger
to hide   to place something where no-one can see it
jealous   wanting what someone else has
leaf(*s.*) **leaves**(*pl.*)   the flat green part of a flower or a tree
mistake   doing something wrong
mud   very wet earth
net   a bag made of material put together with small spaces: for example, a bag used to catch fish
pig   the animal that gives bacon
pipe   a long piece of wood or grass, that can make music

plant   something that grows out of the land
pot   a round bowl
proud   to feel very pleased with yourself
punishment   the act of doing something in return for wrongs; for example, going to prison is a punishment
sharp   very fine, like a knife; you can *cut* with something that is sharp
skin   the outside part of an animal or person
snake   a long thin animal that loses its skin
spear   a long bar with a sharp end, used to kill
tower   a very tall building
valley   the low part between mountains
voice   the sound made by people or animals
well   a deep place where water is kept
wing   the part that helps a bird to fly
yolk   the yellow part of an egg

Glossary of Names
Artemis   the Greek name for the young woman who was the moon
Chang-o   the woman in the Chinese story, who went to the moon
Diana   the Roman name for the young woman who was the moon
Hina   the woman in the story of the Tahiti people who went to live in the moon

Kamonu   the first man in the story of the Barotse people of Zambia

Nasilele   the wife of the Maker in the story of the Barotse people. When she went to the sky, she became the moon

Nyambi   the Maker in the Barotse story. When he went to the sky, he became the sun

Qat   the Maker in the story of the Oceanic people of Banks Island

Ra   the Egyptian King who went to the sky and became the sun